JULIA
DONALDSON

illustrated by

SARA
OGILVIE

The Detective Dog

GODWINBOOKS   Henry Holt and Company • New York

There once was a dog with a keen sense of smell.
She was known far and wide as Detective Dog Nell.
Sniff, sniff, sniff! Time after time,
Nell the detective solved crime after crime.

Who threw the hazelnuts down from the trees?

Who took the honey away from the bees?

Who left the poo on the new gravel path?

How did the spider get into the bath?

Sniff, sniff, sniff! With a wag of her tail,
Nell the detective was hot on the trail.

Nell shared her house with a person called Peter,
A very nice child, though he could have been neater.
And six-year-old Peter was one of those boys
Who kept on misplacing his clothes and his toys.
Sniff, sniff, sniff! Nose to the ground—
These are the things that Detective Dog found:

The bus in the bowl and
the book in the bed,

The sock in the sofa,
  the shoe in the shed,

The tumbledown teddy, the bounce-away ball.

Nell the detective discovered them all.

Now, Nell did detection from Tuesday till Sunday
But did something totally different each Monday.
She found Peter's bag and she tracked down her lead,
Then set off for school, where she heard children read.

The children loved reading their stories to Nell,
And Nell loved to listen—and also to smell.
Sniff, sniff, sniff! Mixed in the air
Were Play-Doh and pudding and newly washed hair,
The crusts in the trash and the coats on the hooks,
But the best smell of all was the smell of the books.

Books about dinosaurs, books about knights,
Books about planets and meteorites,

Books about princes who turned into frogs,
Books about dragons—and books about dogs!

But then came a Monday when all was not well.
Nell sniffed the air, and she smelled the wrong smell.

Into the classroom the two of them hurried
And found Mr. Jones looking terribly worried.
He tugged at his hair and he let out a sigh.
Peter looked 'round and he started to cry.
Sniff, sniff, sniff! What was going on?
"The books!" cried out Peter. "The books are all gone!"

Nell gave a growl when she heard the bad news
But then started sniffing and searching for clues.

Sniff, sniff, sniff! On the bookshelf, a cap!
The thief must have dropped it, the terrible chap.

Nell sniffed the cap, then she tugged on the lead,
And, *Woof*! She was off at astonishing speed.

Everyone followed Detective Dog Nell.
She stopped at the traffic light. What could she smell?

Sniff, sniff, sniff! Haddock and hay,
Pizza and penguins, and farther away,
The smell of the thief and—how very exciting—
Thousands of pages, all covered in writing!

Then, *Woof!* They were off, with no time for a stop,
Past the farm . . . and the zoo . . . and the Fry & Pie shop.

They raced through a field (where the rabbits smelled good),
Then over a golf course and into a wood.

FRY & PIE

OPEN

They thrashed through the undergrowth, leafy and dense,
Till they came to a gate in an old wooden fence.
Then Nell started growling and pricked up an ear.
She barked, and the bark meant *The thief is in here*.

They flung the gate open, and Peter cried, "Look!"
For there sat a man with his nose in a book.
There were many more books poking out of a sack,
And the children yelled,
    "Those are OUR books! Give them back!"

Sniff, sniff, sniff! The book thief looked sad.
"I'm sorry," he sniffled. "I know I've been bad.
Stealing is wrong—but I just meant to borrow.
I was planning to give all the books back tomorrow."

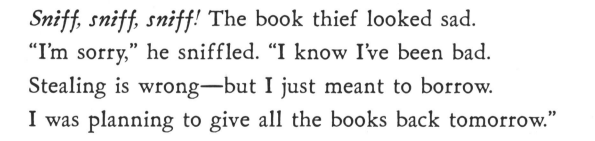

To borrow? To borrow? Nell pricked up an ear.
She barked, and the bark meant *I've got an idea.*

Then, *Woof!* She was off, and away they all sped,
Including the book thief (who told them, "I'm Ted").
Sniff, sniff, sniff! They raced through the wood
And over the field where the rabbits smelled good.

They panted and puffed past the Fry & Pie shop,
The zoo, and the farmyard with never a stop

(Except to retrieve Peter's scarf and his ball,
Which someone had thoughtfully placed on a wall)

Till they came to a building with doors open wide.
And what did they see when they all went inside?

Thousands of books, from the floor to the ceiling.
The books gave the thief the most heavenly feeling.
He gazed in amazement. "Where am I?" he said,
And Peter replied, "In the library, Ted.
You can join if you want to—there isn't a fee,
And then you can take lots of books out for free."

CURL UP WITH A BOOK

So Ted has a lovely new library card,
And he sits reading books in his little backyard.

And when it's a Monday, Detective Dog Nell
Visits the school with the wonderful smell.

Sniff, sniff, sniff! With a faraway look,
She smells and she listens to book after book:

Books about dinosaurs, books about knights,
Books about planets and meteorites,
Books about princes who turn into frogs,
Books about dragons, and books about dogs . . .

All the old books, and a new one as well:
The story of daring Detective Dog Nell.

For Patricia and Kyna —J. D.
For Margaret —S. O.

Henry Holt and Company, *Publishers since 1866*
Henry Holt® is a registered trademark of Macmillan Publishing Group, LLC
175 Fifth Avenue, New York, NY 10010 • mackids.com

Library of Congress Control Number: 2017957737
ISBN 978-1-250-15676-1

Our books may be purchased in bulk for promotional, educational, or business use. Please contact your
local bookseller or the Macmillan Corporate and Premium Sales Department at
(800) 221-7945 ext. 5442 or by e-mail at MacmillanSpecialMarkets@macmillan.com.

First published in the United Kingdom in 2016 by Macmillan Children's Books
First American edition, 2018
Printed in China by Wing King Tong Paper Products Co. Ltd., Shenzhen City, Guangdong Province

1 3 5 7 9 10 8 6 4 2